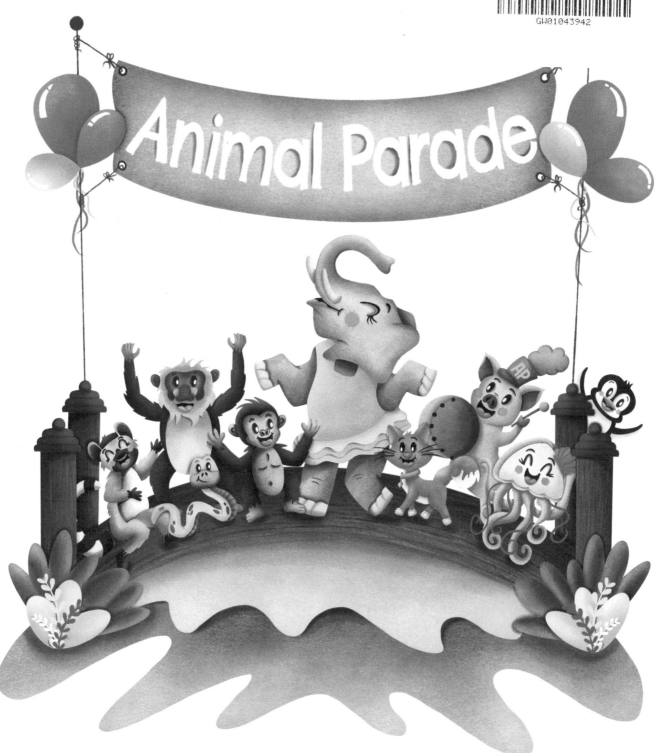

# Animal Parade

Written by Emily Dyson
Illustrated by Laura Chaggar

Printed in the United Kingdom
First Printing, 2019
ISBN: Print (Soft Cover): 978-1-912677-33-7

Published by Purple Parrot Publishing.
www.purpleparrotpublishing.co.uk

For my mischievious monkeys,
**Elizabeth** and **Harriet**.
I hope you always find books to read that make you smile!

With thanks to Mum, Nick, Viv, Jessica and Laura.

Come on down and join us at the animal parade!
The spectacle is wonderful, you will be glad you stayed.
They parade on down the high street if you give them half a chance.
Come and see them march along and creep and jump and dance!

See them all parading through the town without a care.
Come on down and join them, they would love to see you there!

See lively lemurs leaping and the brown bears boogie past.
See lazy lions lolloping, not going very fast.

See mischievous monkeys mambo and the
beautiful birds burst out.
See precocious parrots pirouette whilst crowds
all cheer and shout.

See brilliant baboons balance and the graceful gazelles go.
See gleeful geckos giggle at a joke that they all know.
See sneaky snakes slither and delightful donkeys dance.
See fabulous flamingos frolic by in quite a trance.

See crafty crocodiles creeping, silly sea lions try to swim.
See tiny tamarins tango for a prize they'd like to win!

See the tenacious tortoise traipsing and humongous hippos hurry.
See expressive elephants easing by without a care or worry.

See gentle giraffes jogging and the marvellous meerkats march.
See terrific tigers tiptoe through the big stone arch.

See great gorillas gallop and adventurous aardvarks amble.
See resourceful rodents roaming – near a cat
that's quite a gamble!

See pretty pigs parading and the daft dogs dart along.
See happy horses hopping, singing to their favourite song.

See skilful skylarks skipping and tremendous t-rex train.
See tireless terrapins tap dance with a top hat and a cane.

See zany zebras zigzag, kind koalas conga by.
See crazy cows cartwheeling, oh yes, they can really fly!

See cheerful cheetahs charging and
triumphant toucans twirl.
See robust rhinos running. Oh no!
Watch out for that girl!

See heart-warming hedgehogs hurdle
and the joyful jellyfish jive.
See kooky kangeroos kicking,
big bees buzzing to their hive.

See wonderful wallabies waltzing, splendid spiders spinning past.
See angry apes advancing, cross that they've been left till last!

Yes, come on down and join us at the animal parade!
The spectacle is wonderful, you will be glad you stayed.
They parade on down the high street if you give them half a chance.
Come and see them march along and creep and jump and dance!

See them all parading through the town without a care.
Come on down and join them, they would love to see you there!

# Fantastic Facts
## Did you know?

An aardvark can eat up to 50000 ants in one night. It catches them with its very long, sticky tongue and swallows them whole.

A grizzly bear's bite is strong enough to crush a bowling ball!

The cheetah is the fastest land animal on the planet. they can reach speeds of up to 120kph (75mph).

A male donkey is called a jack and a female is called a jenny.

Baby elephants suck their trunks for comfort like babies suck their thumbs.

Elephants can't jump!

Flamingos are not pink when they are born, they are grey. Their diet contains a natural pink dye that makes their feathers turn pink.

Both giraffes and humans have 7 vertebrae in their necks, but a giraffe's vertebrae can be up to 25.5cm long.

Kangeroos are known for boxing, if they can't push their opponent over with their front paws they kick them with their powerful back legs.

Koala's have fingerprints almost identical to human ones. There are even reported cases of koala's fingerprints confusing forensics at crime scenes!

All species of lemur originate from the island of Madagascar.

Lions have excellent night vision and usually hunt at night.

A group of parrots is called a pandemonium.

Emperor Penguins are the world's largest penguins growing up to 100cm tall.

Rhino horns are made out of keratin, the same as your hair and nails!

Snakes can't close their eyes, they don't have eyelids!

Tigers have striped skin as well as striped fur. Each tiger stripe pattern is unique!

Zebra's sleep standing up!